Kids Stories Book About Minecraft

D1502889

A Collection of Marvelous Minecraft Short Stories For Children

Acquire Complete **ULTIMATE** Book Collection!

Minecraft: Ultimate Book of Secrets

Minecraft: Ultimate Building Book

Minecraft: Ultimate Building Ideas

Minecraft: Ultimate Redstone Book

Master Minecraft Together With Us!

Minecraft: Ultimate Book of Traps

Minecraft: Ultimate Survival Book

Minecraft: Ultimate Book of Battle

Minecraft: Ultimate Book of Seeds

Explore Our Marvelous Minecraft Novels

Mysterious Smile of Herobrine

Unbelievable Adventures Of Steve

Incredible Tale Of Steve

Defender of The Ender

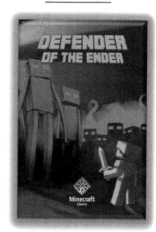

Licence Notes

Minecraft
Library

Table of Content

The Troller

Stonemann had just finished setting up his world and was inviting

friends to come try it out. They all seemed to like it and asked if they

could invite some of their friends to play on it and Stonemann said it

was ok. He thought the more people he had play it the better it would be.

"This castle will work perfect for a battle arena!"

Stonemann Built all sorts of buildings and cities for people to play, live,

or fight in. He even added in a fishing camp with a lighthouse for those who wanted to fish and see at night.

"Cake, this is Cake City!"

"This should make a nice fishing camp."

After everybody was in the game and having a good time, Stonemann

started hearing a lot of shouting from the people in his party. Somebody had been pouring lava all over everything and planting TNT traps in

players houses, Stonemann had to find out who and put a stop to it!

"WHAT?? WHY WOULD SOMEBODY DO THAT?!"

Not sure how to go about finding and catching a troller Stonemann had

a hard job to do, even more than he had imagined when he returned to his house and saw that the troller had found him.

"MY HOUSE!?!"

Very unhappy that they had messed with his house, Stonemann

set out to find just who it was that was trolling people in his world

and ruined his house. After talking to the ones he knew wouldn't

do it, they set out with a plan to catch the troller in the act and

deal with him!

After building some new houses, Stonemann knew that the troller wouldn't be able to resist pouring lava on them or using a flint and steel on them. They made them in such a way that everybody could see them so that the troller wouldn't be able to resist leaving them be.

"There, now we will wait until the troller tries to blow them up"

Since it had been a little while Stonemann and his friends decided it was time to check up on their trap. As they approached the houses they saw smoke coming from the area, running to get there and catch him in the act, Stonemann was happy with what he saw!

"AHA! We got him guys, we caught him in the act!"

The troller was pouring lava all over the houses when Stonemann and his friends came over the hill, seeing them coming he didn't know what to do. The troller turned out to be a player that joined the party from a friend inviting him, his name was Krill. After catching Krill in the act of trolling Stonemann asked him why he was trolling.

"Why are you trolling us man?!?"

Krill didn't know what to say to them and just looked around.

Krill looked at what he had done

Since Krill was there and had lava in his hand Stonemann asked him again why he had done it. Krill dropped the lava bucket under water and told them. "This wasn't me! I was swimming in the water and saw lava falling and came up to look!" Stonemann explained that they had caught him doing it and that he was going to be banned from the world forever. Krill wasn't happy to hear that. "NO! Don't do that maaannn. I'll help you rebuild everything I promise! Just don't ban me!" But Stonemann wasn't listening to him. "You trolled after you promised to help me build my world better and I let you in. I'm not listening to you this time Krill, I'm banning you!" After Krill had been banned Stonemann and the others started working on a house that they could all live in together so that if another troller got on they would be able to catch him really easy. Stonemann gave everybody a few diamonds for helping catch the troller and building the house with him.

"There we go, the house is done!"

The house they built looked amazing! Stonemann liked it so much he decided to make it the capital of the world and there they lived in the minecraft world, safe from trollers forever!

Stopping the Raiding Irongurl

Josh was just getting home from school, and after a long day at school he wanted nothing more than to play some minecraft online. He grabs a drink then heads for the world of minecraft. Josh decides to join a factions survival game with some friends and starts working on building

up his supplies. He needs Iron, Gold, Wood, and most important…

Diamonds! After playing for a few hours he finally finds three diamonds

and immediately mines them and goes to hide them in his faction.

"Here we are! Home sweet home."

After arriving at the faction house and looking through all the chests,

Josh decided that putting his stuff in with the faction stuff wasn't the

best idea. He wasn't being selfish, he just didn't want the other players taking his stuff that he had worked so hard to find!

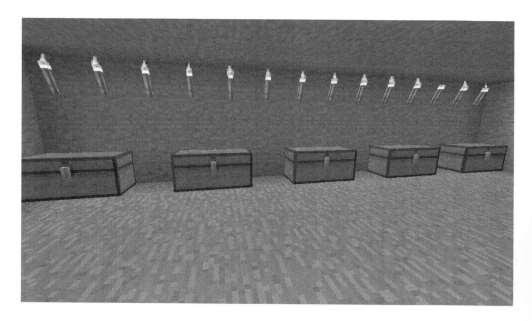

"They have all these chests but I don't want to lose my diamonds."

So after think about it for a while Josh decided it would be best to build

a chest for himself and hide it. Not sure where to put it Josh started

looking around for a spot, then he after going inside one more time he

had the perfect spot! "OF COURSE!" He shouted. Josh grabbed his pickaxe and started digging until he thought he had gone far enough.

"Nobody will think to look UNDER the big chests for another chest!"

Happy with his work, Josh went out to do some more exploring and to find more diamonds. What Josh didn't see when he left was Irongurl and her faction members, Irongurl had seen Josh find the diamonds and wanted them for her faction. Irongurl and her members waited until they were sure he and all the other members were gone and ran in to raid their base. Josh was in the middle of killing a big group of cows and pigs when he saw the message in the chat. "ALL MEMEBRS BACK TO THE BASE!!!! WE GOT RAIDED!!!" Josh looked in horror, his only thoughts were about his diamonds and if they had been found. When

Josh arrived at the base he couldn't believe they had been hit this hard

by raiders.

"How could somebody do this to our base???!!!"

Josh and the members of his faction were trying their best to figure out

who it was that could have done this to them. Then one of the members

said "LOOK HERE!"

"Ok guys, now we know who did it."

After finding out who had raided their house Josh remembered seeing an

Irongurl following him when he had found the diamonds. Josh ran inside

to find his chest and see if the diamonds were still there.

"Oh no... hopefully they didn't see it there and just broke thing."

As Josh worked to get rid of the lava flowing around his chest he hoped

that the diamonds would still be there. Finally he made it to the chest

and opened it slowly, hoping to find diamonds, gold, and iron in it. What he found instead made him so mad!

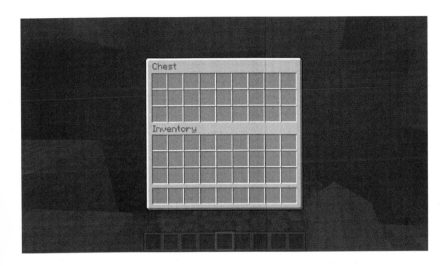

"Let's attack them back!!!!"

Josh told the leaders. "We should attack Irongurl and get all our stuff

back and take Irongurls stuff as well!" The members all agreed with him

so the leaders decided to have a meeting about if they should attack them

or not. They decided to send a spy into Irongurls faction and find out

how many members they have and to open the door for them. Josh had a

friend who wasn't in a faction yet so he asked him to join Irongurls

group. Golemsmasher wasn't new to faction raids, in fact he had led

some himself on another server, so when Josh asked him for help he was

appy to. Golemsmasher messaged Irongurl asking to join her faction.

"Hey Irongurl, I am trying to join a faction and this noob group won't let me join because they don't like that I steal stuff or raid other peoples houses…. Would you let me join yours?" Irongurl knew which group he had tried to join since it was the only 'no raiding' faction here, so she welcomed him into the faction and showed him around the place.

"This is our base, don't steal anything or ill kick you out!"

After he figured out how many people were at the base Golemsmasher messaged Josh saying it was just Irongurl right now and to attack now!

As Josh and the others entered the base they were amazed at how good it

looked.

"Wow! Look at the way they made the entrance."

As they were starting to climb the last ladder Golemsmasher messaged

Josh and told him to wait for twenty seconds then attack! Josh told

everybody what to do when they go in and then they attacked, up the

ladder they climbed one by one trying to get in as fast as they could go.

When they reached the top and saw how good the place looked, they

couldn't wait to fill it with lava and ruin it like theirs had been ruined.

"Look at this place! LET'S DO THIS GUYS!"

They charged in and started breaking everything and taking the good

stuff. Josh knew where his stuff would be so he ran straight through to

Irongurls room and with the help of Golemsmasher he managed to make

her teleport back to the spawn point and leave. Now that she was gone,

Josh took back his iron, gold, and diamonds.

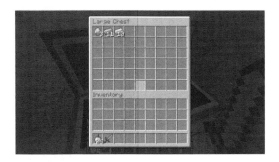

"There they are!"

Josh was just grabbing his diamonds when he heard them call for

everyone to leave so they could dump lava everywhere.

"That will teach them not to mess with us!"

Josh was happy how things had turned out but he thought there as one more thing he could do. On his way out Josh thought. "I'm going to make sure that they know to never mess with us again!"

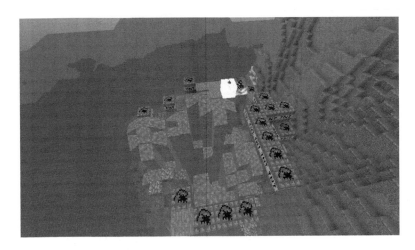

"HAHA! This will teach them not to mess with us!"

After Josh made sure the TNT exploded he teleported back to his faction to celebrate with everybody! While celebrating Josh got a message from rongurl saying. "I'm sorry I took your diamonds but pleaaasseeee don't break our base please!" Josh couldn't believe that she would break their base and make fun of them but didn't want her base broken and begged them not to! After thinking about it Josh felt sorry for her, yes she had broken their base but it was only a small one and pretty new. The base they had was huge and amazing, so he messaged her back telling her he would help fix it. After they finished working together on fixing both bases the two factions joined and became one, Irongurls faction was the raiding party for when it was time for war and Josh and the original group were the resource gatherers. As it came time for Josh to go to sleep he thought about how fast the day had gone by and couldn't wait for tomorrow when he could leave school and get back on minecraft!

Alex versus the Ender Dragon

Alex was enjoying the new world he found herself in, there was plenty of animals for food, plenty of trees for wood, and he even ran across a village to live in that had plenty of people to visit with. Yes everything seemed fine to her but they were starting to get a little boring, she wanted something exciting and new to try. One night when the village was having a campfire cook out, the village elder told a story about the grand Enderdragon and how he flew through the air and ruled over the land until the mighty warrior came and defeated him. Steve had come one day and sent the dragon into the end portal, but one day the dragon would return and Steve was no longer around to save them. Alex hearing this new she had found new exciting adventure; Defeat the Enderdragon for good!

"The Dragon will return and when he does his anger will be terrible!"

The next morning Alex asked the elder where the portal was located that

the Enderdragon was said to come out of, but he told her that there was

no telling where the new portal would appear just that it would and soon.

Alex was still curious about him so she asked how he was defeated the

first time and why Steve disappeared. "When Steve defeated him, how

did he do it? And why did he leave afterwards?" The elder wasn't sure

how to respond so he told her the conversation that he had with Steve

before he left. "Steve was an adventurer, much like you, and he was

ready to go on an adventure. The day Steve prepared to go was the day the Ender Dragon came to our village…" As he said the last words his gaze drifted into space remembering a time long ago. "Steve took his sword and waited for the dragon to come around a corner so he could jump on his back. As the EnderDragon did Steve jumped as far as he could and landed on the Dragons back. While Steve battled it, the Ender Dragon caused so much destruction that after it was finished it took us almost three years to clean up the mess."

"Come look at this Alex."

The elder finished the story and then pointed to a mountain outside the village. "Steve left his sword in that mountain after he struck the final blow to the Dragon. We have never gone to find it and Steve said to leave it there for the next adventurer to claim if they can defeat the Ender Dragon once and for all."

"That mountain was created during Steve and the Ender Dragons Battle."

So Alex started training hard with her sword and bow so that when the dragon came she could protect the people who lived there from him, but day after day went by and no portal could be found or dragon seen. One day during her archery training the elder came to see Alex, he had come to tell her the news she had been waiting for.

"Alex I need to talk to you."

"The signs that show when the Ender Dragon returns are all happening, he will be here soon!" Alex was so excited when she heard this; she went to grab her armor, sword, and bow. The village elder followed her explaining how dangerous this was going to be and as he was finishing there was an earthquake and a loud explosion. Alex went outside to see what was going on and she couldn't believe what she saw.

"Is that the Ender Dragons portal?"

The elder knew what was coming so he warned the village to flee once again from the Dragons wrath. Alex however, didn't run away but straight towards the portal to go head to head with the Ender Dragon and kill it once and for all! Alex took up her bow, ready to fire if the Dragon came out of the portal to destroy the village. As Alex got closer and closer, there was a sound like thunder, and without warning…

"I've got to save those villagers from the Dragon!"

The Ender dragon had come and nobody was ready for his quick attack.

Alex took aim with her bow and started shooting at the Ender Dragon.

Arrow after arrow Alex let fly, but the dragon wasn't taking any damage it seemed. Alex knew what she had to do, she ran for the mountain where Steve had left his sword, for any hero worthy of defeating the Ender Dragon would need it.

"Steve's sword must be in that chest!"

Alex saw the chest where she figured the sword was stored in but with

lava all around it she wasn't sure how she would get to it. After thinking

about it Alex dumped a bucket of water on the lava to turn it into

cobblestone so she could walk right over it, but when the water hit the

lava it instantly turned into steam instead of changing the lava. Alex

decided that the only way to get there was to jump and so she positioned

herself, with a running start she jumped with all she had towards the

chest. As she got closer to the ledge Alex realized she wasn't going to

make it, she reached out and grabbed hold of the wall around the chest and pulled herself up. When she opened the chest and took Steve's

sword she couldn't believe what happened; the sword made her fly!

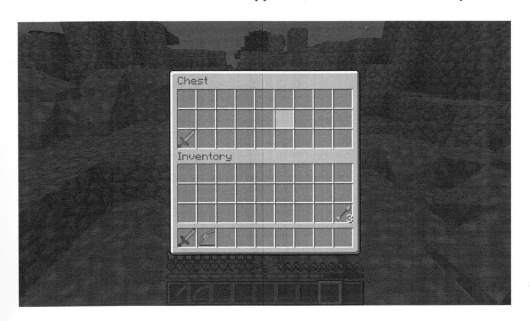

"Yes! Steve's sword is actually here... whoaaaaa!"

When she took off flying, Alex headed straight for the Ender Dragon.

With her new weapons she knew she could defeat him for good this time

and save everyone in the village. The Ender Dragon saw her coming and

turned straight at her, flying closer and closer Alex prepared to fight him

with all of her might. 'CLANG... CLING...' Alex swung her sword at

the dragon as he flew by 'RAAAWWWWRRRR' The Dragon felt her

sword hit him and was confused why this little human was standing to fight him. The battle between Alex and the Ender Dragon went on for 5 days and neither of them grew tired or hungry, they just kept fighting. Alex wanted to protect the village and its people. The Ender Dragon wanted to return to the way things were before; king over the entire world with everyone fearing his power! The villagers watched as Alex fought bravely to protect them day after day. On the seventh day of fighting the Ender Dragon had taken enough damage he knew he was going to lose, so to protect himself he flew as high as he could go and disappeared.

Alex landed and said to the villagers. "He will be back and we need to be ready this time! Set up giant bows to shoot at him while we battle next time!" The elder told everyone to get to work on the bows and to make the arrows out of all the diamonds they had left. Alex asked the elder how long Steve had battled the Dragon before he trapped it in the end portal. "Steve and the Ender Dragon battled for only three hours before he trapped it in the portal, but Steve wasn't fighting to kill it like you are." He explained. Alex knew this was going to be a hard fight but she didn't think it would be this hard. After listening to the elder tell more about Steve's battle with the Dragon she went to get some sleep before the Dragon returned. On the third day after the Ender Dragon disappeared there came a sound in the distance.

'RAAAAAAAWWWWWWWRRRRRR' The Dragon had returned to

fight and so every villager ran to their bows ready to fire at Alex'

command. Alex grabbed Steve's sword and took off to meet the Dragon

above the village for the final battle between them. As Alex swung her

sword over and over she gave the signal to fire on him. Out of the

village came a cloud of arrows, so many were flying towards the Dragon

that when they reached him he had no place to hide or fly. Alex took this

chance and charged him with her sword ready to strike, and strike it did.

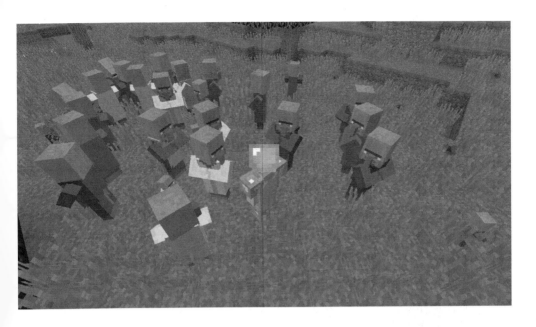

he sword struck the Ender Dragon in the chest as the arrows hit from

very direction. With a loud, thundering sound the Ender Dragon

xploded into a million pieces.

"It's finally over! We have won!"

Alex watched from a nearby cloud as the Dragon disappeared in a puff

of smoke. The villagers started to celebrate as Alex came down from her

cloud to return Steve's sword to the chest she had claimed it from

something amazing happened; all the lava turned into obsidian and a

glass floor appeared above the lava around the chest.

"WOW! Look at that, it's amazing!!"

Now that Alex had returned the sword and destroyed the Ender Dragon it was time to fix the village. Alex and the villagers worked together all day for weeks and after all the hard work and defending against zombie and skeleton attacks they finished the village! Alex even had the idea to turn the Ender Dragons portal into a new hot tub for the village so they could soak in the water during the winter and not be freezing.

"We are finally done fixing the village!"

Alex was finished working and decided it was time to move on, the villagers were safe and she wanted another adventure. So she collected some obsidian, grabbed a flint and steel, and then headed out to build a nether portal for her next adventure! She finished the nether portal, gathered her armor and weapons, said her goodbyes to the villagers, and then stepped into the portal and the unknown world beyond.

Alex explores the nether

Alex stepped down from the nether portal, sword in her hand ready for anything that would come... Or so she thought. When Alex walked out of the portal something sounded odd, so she went around the corner to see what it was and it caught her off guard.

"Wither skeletons... capturing bats??"

Wither skeletons, the skeleton that if it touches you it causes you to rot way, was capturing bats for pets. Bats indeed, the Wither skeleton had ready captured so many bats Alex wasn't sure how to get out of there.

Alex finally made her way out of the Withers bat cave and into the

nether world, what she saw now was even more unbelievable!

"A village... in the nether?!?"

A village had spawned in the nether and Alex was going to find out how it had,

having never heard of it happening before she was really curious. Alex walked

around the village for a while trying to find any clues as to who it could have been

that spawned this village, after a short time he found what she was looking for.

Now Alex knew who had spawned the village but the one who had done it was

someone that Alex feared more than any other thing in minecraft... The

ENDERMAN KING!

"Enderman King is in the nether... That is not good!"

Alex knew the name 'Enderman King' all too well. Alex had seen his handy work in the overworld, he had stolen things from her house and destroyed her farm too. Enderman King was the known enemy of anybody who dared venture into his world, he would appear and disappear without a trace. His most known and feared feature was the sound he would make should you look at him; it struck fear into the heart of the bravest of adventures. Alex however, was going to find him and beat him! She would be the first to outsmart the great Enderman King and defeat him! So Alex started preparing for a battle with the

Enderman King, knowing it would be a difficult one and that she would

need to keep an eye on his village for when he spawned she decided to

build a house under one of his houses. As she prepared to build however,

she heard a noise that made her back go stiff... Enderman were

spawning everywhere around the village!

"I need to hide and fast!"

"I need to hide and fast!" she thought. Alex ran into a house and closed

the door hoping to stay hidden from the eyes of the endermen, as she

dropped to the ground inside an enderman walked by the window

checking to make sure everything was alright in the Kings village. After they had finished their check of the village and left, Alex walked around the village talking to the villagers asking them questions about the Enderman King. "Why did he spawn a village in the middle of the nether?" She asked. The villagers told her that if they couldn't grow food then they would starve, but the King has the endermen bring food to them from the over world so they can eat but only if they obey him. Alex didn't like the sound of that and was going to lead them out of the village through her portal and to the overworld so they could build a new home, but as got the gate, Alex couldn't remove the fence piece locking them in so they were trapped until she figured out how to get rid of it.

"It won't break! We are stuck until I can figure this out."

Alex paced back and forth inside, trying to figure out how to break that fence post blocking the door. She thought about using TNT to blow it up, but decided that wouldn't work since the endermen would hear it. Then she thought about melting it with lava, but once again she would have to get out to reach the lava. Idea after idea Alex couldn't think of a way to break it with what she had. Finally something came to her. "If I can kill an enderman while he is walking around the village I could use his pearl to teleport out and get some lava!" She was thinking, but as she thought about it an even better idea came to mind.

"We could use the iron golems to fight the endermen and win, then use their pearls to teleport out of here and go to the overworld!" The villagers weren't too sure about this idea but they didn't have any better ones so they decided to use it. The next morning when the endermen came to bring breakfast, Alex and the villagers were ready for them. The first enderman to enter the village was jumped by the Iron golems and some villagers; they took him down without any trouble.

"Get him!"

The Iron golems used their attacks against the enderman to throw him into the air, the villagers waited for him to land so they could get a hit or two in themselves. After defeating the first enderman the villagers and golems went back into hiding, waiting for the next enderman to arrive. Seeing the villagers' attack the enderman on sight, Alex knew they could do this. She ran into her house and waited for the enderman to show.

Alex was lying in wait for her enderman to show up and when he did,

she jumped him!

"AHA!! I've got you now!"

The enderman was not happy that he was being attacked by a little

human; he attacked back with everything he had to kill Alex. Alex

however, equipped with a diamond sword had the upper hand and struck

him over and over, after one final blow from her sword the enderman

was finished. After Alex won the fight, she took the endermans pearl as her own!

"There we go! Now we need to get some for the rest of the villagers!"

Alex ran outside after picking up the pear, there was a noise coming

from the village like she hadn't heard before. As she walked out the door

she was amazed at what she saw. The villagers, after seeing how easy it

was to defeat the endermen, attacked with full force and used their Iron

golems to defeat them. Alex joined in the battle to aid the villagers and

hopefully win so they could defeat the Enderman King once and for all.

It took a long time but, afterwards Alex and the villagers were able to

defeat the endermen!

"Get em!! We can do this guys!"

After the battle was over, they collected all the ender pearls they could find and counted them up, they had just enough for everyone to escape to the overworld!

"We are out! Come on we need to get out of the nether."

Alex was the first to use an ender pearl so the villagers knew what to do, after getting everyone out and walking through the nether portal Alex knew they were safe. Once they were through the gate Alex did a head count to make sure everybody had made it out, seeing they were all safe she took them to the nearby village for their new home.

"This is your new home guys!"

he villagers couldn't believe their eyes! Vegetables everywhere, houses lade out of wood, and even a swimming pool! They were as happy as ley could be so they had a party, but something happened that night at none of them expected.

"The enderman are attacking us here?!?"

The Enderman King did not like his villagers being stolen while he was away and he really didn't like that they had killed all of the enderman guards. He brought his entire army to bring the villagers back and kill the one who had helped them escape! Alex was a quick thinker, so she turned around and headed for the blacksmith to get the iron stored there. When she returned with it she created an army of golems to defend the villagers from the Enderman King and his army.

"It's raining! Enderman can't stand the rain!"

When Alex led the Iron golems to battle the Enderman King and his

army, something wonderfully unexpected happened. "IT'S RAINING!!"

The villagers shouted. Rain indeed, a storm had come as they normally

do at evening and with perfect timing too, enderman hate the rain and

cannot stand to be in it. SO while it rained and the Enderman King and

his army ran for cover, Alex, the villagers, and the golems attacked! The

enderman King was just about to teleport to his castle when Alex struck

him with her sword, causing him to drop his pearl and be stuck in the

rain and battle. Alex seeing that he was trapped didn't let up; she swung her sword again and again! Finally, after a few hours of chasing him around and fighting when he was stuck, Alex defeated the Enderman King!

The Enderman King falls in battle, defeated by Alex

The remaining endermen, seeing their king fall retreated into the forest, never to bother the villagers again. When the battle was over and the villagers were gathering around Alex to celebrate she told them. "All you have to do is believe in yourself no matter what, and there is nothing you can't do with the help of friends and the courage to do what is needed!" The villagers thanked her as she packed her things to leave; it was time for another adventure!

Getting started in a new world

Alex was an adventurous girl, she loved exploring, climbing mountains, mining deep into the earth, and pretty much anything you could think of. So when she found herself in a new world full of unexplored lands, mountains, and even ravines, Alex knew she was going to have a lot of fun!

"Look at all the places to explore!"

"The first thing I need to do is build a small house to explore from." She said to herself. So Alex set out to gather all the blocks she would need to build, while gathering she decided she wanted a granite house with a birchwood ceiling. She also needed food so she killed rabbits for the meat and leather, and sheep for their wool and mutton. As night came, Alex had finished her house, gathered some food, and built a bed.

"This will do juuust fine."

Looking around outside making sure she was safe, Alex went inside to

sleep until morning.

"Time to sleep, I have a big day tomorrow!"

When morning came Alex was ready to go mining and exploring. She

was so excited in fact, that she almost forgot to close the door when she left the house.

Having closed the door Alex took off on her first adventure; to find a mine! She didn't have to go very far it turned out, just a few blocks behind her house there was a hole in the ground to a very large cave for her to explore! "Alright! Here I gooooo." She said as she jumped down the hole.

"This is the perfect place!"

As Alex entered the caves at the bottom she found lots of coal and

granite inside. Farther and farther she went into the cave, almost to the

bottom Alex found iron!

"IRON!! Now I can make my chest piece and have some protection!"

When she arrived back at the house Alex put the iron ore in the furnace to smelt it down as soon as possible. After she started the furnace and put the stuff she collected in the chest, she got ready for bed. Morning came with a knock on the door… a knock? Alex jumped out of bed at the sound of knocking on her door. She wasn't sure who would be knocking so she grabbed her sword and went to investigate. As she rounded the corner of her house she was shocked at what she saw!

Zombies attack the house

Zombies were attacking her house in numbers, so Alex did the only thing she knew to do... ATTACK! She leapt into battle with the zombies and swung her sword with all her might, hoping to defeat them and protect her home. After defeating the zombies however, creepers started coming to attack! One by one they blew up creating holes in the ground. Alex seeing this knew what would happen to her house if they reached it so she charged them head on to prevent them from reaching it!

"GET OUT OF MY HOUSE ZOMBIES!!!!!"

"That was too close! Oh no! More zombies are attacking!"

After dealing with the creepers Alex saw no end to the zombies attacking her house. So she went inside and waited for the sun to come out and burn the zombies. Safe inside, Alex listened to the sound of zombies, skeleton archers, and creepers trying to get in her house. Hours went by but still no sun and the attacks kept coming, Alex wasn't sure how much more she could take of the sounds. Deciding she had enough she picked up her sword and charged outside to defeat the zombies. Finishing the last zombie and chasing the creepers away, Alex was happy to see the sun coming up over the hills. Once the morning sun was in the sky Alex decided it was time for a nap.

"It's about time the sun came up! Now I need a nap."

So Alex went inside to nap for a few hours, figuring it would probably

be safer to nap during the day and work at night since she works

underground. After a few hours went by Alex woke up, grabbed her

pickaxe, and headed down into the mine. Down in the mine Alex found

lots of Iron and coal, she also found something she didn't want…

"AH! Get out of here you skeleton archer!"

Alex had run into skeleton archer wandering around the mine, it fired an arrow at her and got her attention with it! She turned to face him and started her attack! CLING… CLASH… TWING… TWANG… The battle lasted for a short time, the archer fired twice before Alex's sword ended its final blows. Alex went back to mining after finishing him off. After collecting everything she had mined it was time to head home.

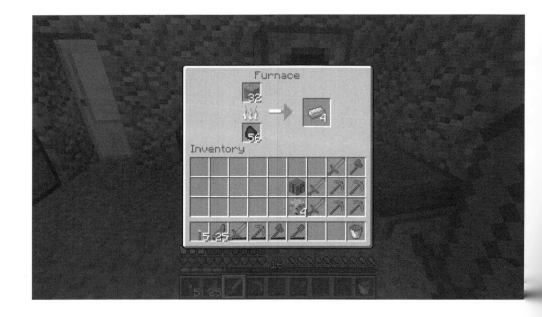

"Look at all the Iron I got!"

Once she got home she started smelting the iron into bars for armor,

tools, buckets, and other things. Alex walked outside to watch the sunset

on another day in Minecraft. Standing there looking out over the hills

Alex said to herself. "I love this place, so many things to do, make,

build, break, and dig."

'As the sun sets on yet another day in Minecraft...'

Alex wanted until the sun was out of sight then turned to watch the

moon com up on the other side. The moon came up over a small forest

in the distance and once again Alex just couldn't imagine living

anywhere else other than Minecraft.

Steve meets Alex

In the world of Minecraft many strange things can happen. Things that you won't be able to explain to your friends and some things that may make you doubt you even saw them. Steve experienced one of those things on a golden summer day, he was walking through the gardens an animals in front of his house, as he walked by the sheep he heard the sound of footsteps coming from behind him. Steve just thought it was the sheep moving around behind him and thought nothing of it, until they started running. Staring in disbelief, Steve rubbed his eyes to make

sure he wasn't dreaming.

Alex was cautious as she approached the new face

A figure approached his house from the nearby woods and walked over

to him. Alex looked at Steve puzzled and asked. "Are you ok?" Steve

couldn't believe his eyes, there was somebody else in the world with

him! Steve realizing he had yet to respond looked at her and said. "Yes

I'm fine. I just wasn't expecting there to be someone else out here, I

thought I was alone in this world." Alex had been thinking the same

thing before meeting him and decided to introduce herself. "My name is

Alex, nice to meet you." Steve responded. "And my name is Steve, it's

nice to meet you too."

As Alex approached him, Steve kept a distance

Steve had so many questions about Alex. Why hasn't he seen her before?

If she had seen him, why didn't she introduce herself? And most

important, how did she get here? All of these questions ran through

Steve's mind as they talked, but he didn't know how to ask them. Not

sure how she would react he left things alone for now so he could

observe her. Steve showed Alex around his village and introduced her to

the villagers; he showed her the farms, the gardens, even the nether

portal he had built.

"This is my nether portal, I use it to get glowstone or netherrock for light."

Alex was impressed; all she had built so far was a dirt house for protection from zombies and skeletons. Steve was happy to have somebody he could actually talk to and not just the villagers. 'How are you doing today bob?' 'huh, huuuuh, hhuuuh' they were always boring and ended after a few questions.

"This is my village!"

Alex was interesting; she was adventurous, creative, and brave. Steve thought it was odd but, they looked a lot alike, they moved a lot alike, and even attacked the same way. This made him curious. "How can we be so much alike and never have run into each other? Wouldn't she have come for place like this, next to the ocean with lots of trees and coal?"

These questions made Steve's head hurt so he decided just to visit with Alex.

Alex wasn't much on talking, she preferred to dig, build, fish, and kill zombies. Steve on the other hand was asking so many questions so fast. Alex tried answering all she could but some of them weren't easy to answer, like. ""How did you get here?" Steve asked that question a lot and she didn't know the answer to it. Finally after three days of questions, Alex said it was her turn to ask questions. Steve agreed, she adn't asked any questions yet so he would let her ask some. Alex asked im. "What is the last thing you remember before waking up in Minecraft?" Steve was about to say it but, when he thought about it he ouldn't remember anything before Minecraft. He woke up in it, slept in worked in it, and built in it. Minecraft was everything he knew.

Alex asked her next question. "Have you ever done something without meaning to? Like digging a block or breaking a tree?" Steve thought about it, he had. He had been digging once in the sand for a garden, while he was digging a block out another block next to it also broke. Alex had one last question she said. "Have you ever been walking around and get the feeling you are being watched, but nothing is there to watch you?" Steve remembered the first day in his new house it felt like he was being watched but he was inside and there was no way to see inside. Wondering about it, Steve got up to look around and make sure they were alone. When he sat back down he explained. "The first day I was in my new house, I was building a second floor and there were no windows or anything. But the entire time I felt like someone was watching me the entire time I was in there." Alex couldn't believe it; she had felt the same thing building her house. "When I was building my house, I went underground to mine some granite for it and felt like someone was sitting there, watching my every move."

eve wondered who could be out there and watching them without

ing seen. Without warning Alex had an iron sword in her hand.

"Whoa whoa whoa, what are you doing?" Steve asked slowly moving away. "I don't have one of these! The only tool I have is a wooden pickaxe!" Alex shouted. Steve then had a steak appear in his hand out of nowhere. "WHOA! Steak just came out of nowhere!!" He was shouting. Alex was too busy trying to figure out where her new sword had come from to hear him. Steve ran outside hoping to see the person or thing that was doing this. When he got outside however, there was nothing there and nobody moving around. Alex snuck out the door afraid that something might attack them and asked Steve if he saw anything out there. Steve was busy running around checking all of his animal pens to make sure they were all there. Everything looked fine until he came to the cows… One was missing!

Steve looked down at the steak in his hand and realized where it had

come from. He ran inside to check his Iron and see if he as missing any,

when he got there two pieces were missing from his chest. Steve set

own and thought for a second. "If we were both sitting here talking,

and one of my cows was killed and cooked then put in my hand, and an

on sword was made for you..." Steve was trying to piece things

together when from outside he heard Alex shouting something. Alex had

stayed behind to look around for a little longer. She found all the things

Steve had made still in their place but something was different and she

didn't know what.

"Steve! Come quick!"

Steve rushed to her side next to the gardens and saw what it was she

shouted for; every wheat plant, watermelon, carrot, and potato had been

picked and replanted. Not sure what was going on, Steve climbed to the

top of his tower to look down at his house. When he reached the top and

looked around everything seemed to be normal, but something wasn't

right. Alex was walking around the village looking at the houses to make

sure they were ok and it all seemed normal to her. While she looked at

the village, Steve stayed in the tower looking around.

Steve looks over his land to make sure everything is ok

Steve finished looking around his land and climbed down from the tower, knowing there was nothing he could do tonight he was going to sleep. Alex was going to return home but Steve said she could take his house and he would sleep in the extra house outside. As Steve lay in bed the thought that someone was out there kept his mind racing with thoughts. Alex wasn't getting anymore sleep than Steve was, how was he here the entire time and she never saw him or anything he had built?

The next morning Steve woke up and was going to check on Alex to see if she was ok but something was odd. When Steve looked around he was back in his bed, but he remembered walking outside to the extra house? Not sure what to make of it he got up to find Alex, but there was no sign of her ever being there. The only thing Steve could remember from last night was a number, a specific number. But knowing the number did him no good if he didn't know what it was for. He thought and thought, paced back and forth trying to come up with some explanation as to what happened last night. Then the number came to him; 1.8.0!

What could this number be or mean? Steve wasn't sure but he knew he didn't like the sound of it, something about it made him scarred. Remembering his mysterious guest Alex, Steve wondered what lay in store for him. Would he have more adventures in Minecraft? Would he build anymore houses? Would he be able to kill zombies, skeletons, creepers, enderman, or spiders anymore? The uncertainty was almost too much for him, so he decided to not worry about it and he went about his day like every other day; he worked, built, gardened, and took care of the villagers. The next morning when the sun was just coming up, something was different… ALEX!

"WHAT?? WHY AM I ALEX??"

Alex indeed, the number Steve had seen earlier was the new update to

Minecraft which turned him into Alex. Not sure what to make of this

Alex decided to leave this house and build another one.

Steve makes a mansion

Steve opened his eyes, stood up off the ground, and started looking around. Minecraft, the world Steve now found himself in was full of creatures and monsters. Steve knew that to survive he would need a house to live in at night so he started building one straight away. As Steve worked on his house, collecting wood for the walls, wool for the carpet, and cobblestone for the furnace he thought. "Why should I only build a small house when I could build a mansion?" So Steve started building a mansion, he collected more wood and cobblestone for his mansion. Days went by as Steve worked on his mansion, but as he got closer and closer to finishing it he noticed things started disappearing. Finally the day had come, his mansion was finished!

"There we go, all done!"

Steve looked at his mansion and was pleased with his work so he went

inside to store some stuff in his chest. Steve had collected a lot of

diamonds and iron.

"There we go!"

Steve went out one day to collect more wood for his house. When he returned that evening he found the door open, he ran inside to inspect his house to make sure nothing had been stolen and when he checked his chest he almost cried.

"Where is all my diamond and iron!?!?"

teve couldn't believe that somebody would take his diamonds from

im, but as he thought about it an even greater question came to mind.

Who could take them? Who out here wants diamonds? Skeletons,

mbies, creepers, and witches don't use them. Enderman have pearls so

ey wouldn't want the diamonds. Who could take them from me?" As

eve tossed this question around in his mind he heard a noise outside.

"HAHAHAHAHAHAHA!!!!"

The ghostly figure appeared and laughed at Steve then vanished just as

quickly as he had come. "Who or what was that??" Steve asked himself

as he ran inside the mansion. Now Steve knew what the thief looked

like, just not who he was. Steve decided to lay some traps on the ground

should he decide to come back and steal some more but before he started

laying them he remembered the way the stranger had appeared. Steve

then realized something. "How do you trap a ghost… that flies??" Not

knowing the answer to this he set out to find someone who did. He went

to the Iron golems in the Hills of the north and asked them, at the

mention of a ghostly figure the golems sent him away. So he traveled to

the village just south of him to ask the village elder but when he mentioned the ghostly figure, once again they sent him away. Steve was

running out of options so he went home to look at the map and find

somewhere else he could go to ask them about the ghostly figure. But as

Steve walked towards his house the figure appeared again!

"HAHAHAHAHAHAHA!"

ou think you can fool me with your little trap? It's a good thing you

ought better of it. "Who are you!?" Steve demanded. "ME?!? You

ant to know MY name?! HAHAHAHAHAHA! You will soon find out

tle man!" The ghostly figure yelled as he disappeared. Steve was

termined to find out who the ghostly figure was, now more than ever!

Steve readied himself for battle with the ghostly figure, one thought

t creeping into his mind. "How do you kill a ghost?" Steve wondered about this but had to keep it out of his mind if he was going to beat him. The ghostly figure watched from the shadows as Steve created weapons and armor, the ghost laughed to himself saying. "Foolish man, you have no idea what you are getting yourself into. Hehehe." Steve was wondering around one day trying to find more iron for his armor when he found a house, a huge house.

"Who does this belong to?? I don't remember it being here earlier?"

And Steve was right, the house, in fact, had not been there before when he was exploring for the perfect place for his mansion. Not sure what it was Steve decided to have a look around.

'Where is the house??"

Steve looked inside and there was no house, just the wall where a house

should be. He walked down to one end of the wall and looked across the

length of the house. When he decided this must have been a house

started by someone else in Minecraft he went to leave but as he did, the

ghostly figure appeared yet again!

"I wonder who built this."

"HAHAHAA! So, you found my house did you? Don't worry, you won't be around long enough to regret it! HAHAHAHA" he said before disappearing once again.

"HAHAHAHA!"

Steve ran home and grabbed his armor and weapons; if this was the ghost's house then this is where he would sleep until he had defeated him! Steve arrived back at the house of the ghost, but the house was gone! Puzzled, Steve retraced his steps and made sure this is where he had found it. "I know it was here." He said to himself. He looked around for the house but couldn't find it until he climbed over a hill near where the ghost's house was.

"That's new. Is that the ghost's new house?"

eve decided to have a look inside and see what the ghost had. As he oroached the house, Steve noticed a note tied to a black disc.

"You think I can't move my house at will? You must be a bigger fool than I thought. How could you hope to defeat me?" Steve noticed a music player sitting in the corner and put the disc inside to play. "Now that you have found my house you should prepare yourself for battle!"

"Hmm I wonder why he left this?"

Steve wasn't sure what was going to happen but he knew it was going to be the end for either him or the ghost, so he ran home to prepare for battle with the ghost! When he got home there was a sign on the door. "Since you will be dead soon I will tell you my name. Herobrine." Now Steve knew the name of the ghost, Herobrine. With this new knowledge

Steve returned to the golems and villagers to ask them for help, but once again they turned him away. However Steve was determined to get the help so he told them of how he planned to defeat Herobrine. "We will lure him into his house and plant an end portal there, hide it under a picture so that when he steps on it he will fall through and into the end. Once he falls in we destroy the portal and he will be trapped there forever!" The golems agreed this was a good idea and could work, but it required the villagers to help. The villagers were not so easily convinced that it would work; they explained that Herobrine can teleport anywhere he wants and doesn't have to have a portal to get out. Steve explained that the end I different than any other place, the only way in or out, even for the ruler of it, the Enderdragon, a portal is the only way out. The village elder decided it was worth a try and that they would aid Steve in the battle against Herobrine. The golems and villagers set to work making the portal in Herobrines house while Steve kept him distracted in battle over at his house.

"There it is, let's do this!"

While Steve was preparing at home to fight Herobrine, he heard a sound that chilled him to the bones, when he turned around he was face to face with Herobrine.

"HAHAHAHA!"

"I know you're here Herobrine! Show yourself coward!"

s quick as he appeared in Steve's house, he vanished again. I know

ou're here Herobrine! Come out and fight me you coward! Herobrine

ouldn't stand this little human calling him, Herobrine a coward! "HA!

ou call me a coward but you are the one using golems and villagers to

ap me inside my own home! You think I can't see what happens in

ere? I know your plan is to trap me in the doorway fool!" Herobrine

arled. Steve was confused, trap in a doorway? He hoped they didn't do

t but he would have to wait and find out. "You think you know my

n do you? HAHAHA! You don't know anything Herobrine!"

Steve yelled back at Herobrine. Steve then jumped out of the window and dashed for Herobrines house, Herobrine saw where he was going and was going to beat him there and set of his trap on Steve.

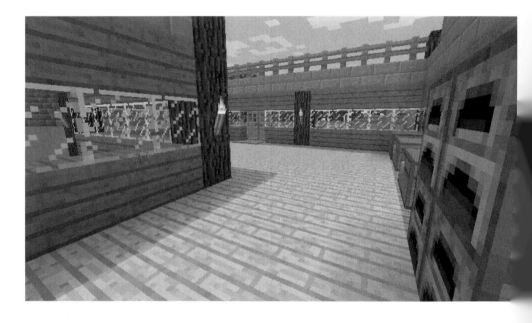

"Why is there no trap on the ground???"

Steve wasn't sure why the trap wasn't set so he prepared to battle Herobrine since the trap wouldn't work. Then the village elder shouted from somewhere. "Stay back Steve!"

"AHA! There it is!"

teve watched as the trap appeared out of thin air and was overjoyed

nowing he didn't have to fight Herobrine after all. Herobrine watched;

urious as to what the lump was that appeared. Steve dared Herobrine to

ow himself and fight. "Come out you coward and fight like a man!"

erobrine was done dealing with this annoying human and charged in

ndly, not realizing that he had been fooled by the villagers. The

lems rushed in the doors using magic to trap Herobrine inside the

use as Steve pushed him closer and closer to the portal. Herobrine leapt into the air over the trap and laughed at their pitiful attempt to trap him.

"You fools think I can be trapped in the nether? HA!"

While he was flying over the portal the villagers released the trap and opened the portal to the end. Realizing he had been tricked, Herobrine tried to move out of the portal, but it was too late. Steve, the golems, and the villagers watched as Herobrine was sucked into the end. Steve quickly broke the portal as soon as Herobrine vanished. "We've done it!" Steve shouted in victory. The villagers and golems started to celebrate as well, that is until they heard the laugh.

"HAHAHAHAHAHAHAHAHAHAHAHAAHA! I am not finished yet,

Steve!"

Herobrines return

Alex was walking around the world she found herself in, looking at all

the buildings and houses. She came to a house that looked strangely

familiar, but she couldn't figure out why. A villager walked up to her

and asked. "Who are you?" Alex was surprised a villager was talking to her since she didn't know they could even talk. "I'm Alex" She responded. "Where is this place and why am I here?" Alex looked at the villager hoping for an answer. "You are in the world of Minecraft, and this is the land that Herobrine once ruled." He responded. "What do you mean 'once ruled'?" She asked. The villager then told her the story of how Steve helped them in trapping the powerful Herobrine. "Herobrine once ruled this land through power and fear. Steve came here one day and was approached by Herobrine with a warning to leave or die. Steve wasn't going to leave the mansion he had just built and he didn't like that we were being treated this way by him."

Alex listened and was amazed that someone took on the great Herobrine

and won. "However." The villager continued. "Herobrine wasn't

defeated. His last words were

'HAHAHAHAHAHAHAHAHAHAHAAHA! I am not finished yet,

Steve!' So we aren't sure if he is gone or not." Alex wandered around

until she found Steve's mansion, it was amazing!

"This is amazing! Steve built this all on his own?"

ex walked inside the mansion and was amazed by what she saw. Steve

I quite the collection of weapons, diamonds, and iron.

"HAHAHAHAHAHAHAHAHA! Steve was first to go and you will be the next if you do not leave!" Alex heard a mysterious voice come out of the air and laugh. She ran out of the house and straight to the villager to tell him all she had heard. When the villager heard this he ran straight home and told the elder. "HEROBRINE HAS RETURNED!" He yelled. After hearing this, the village elder sent word to the golems to warn them that he had indeed returned and his wrath would be terrible. The golems hearing this sent every available soldier they had to defeat him yet again.

Herobrine, the most feared character in all of Minecraft, had returned to get revenge against the golems and villagers. Returning to Steve's mansion to figure out how to defeat him once and for all, the village elder called Alex to come forth.

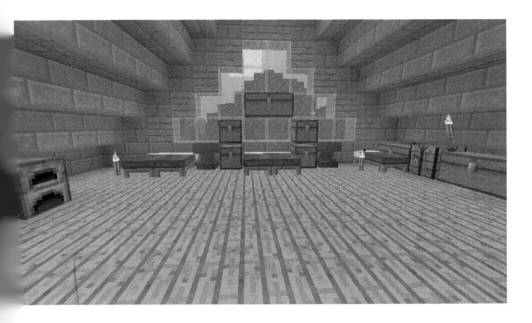

Alex waited in the upstairs bedroom for her call

s Alex waited she looked around Steve's bedroom at all he had

llected. After the elder summoned her, Alex walked downstairs to the

eting and listened as they explained the plan.

Until we are certain that Herobrine has returned we will just have to assume this is a prank that someone is trying to play on us. When out of nowhere.

"HAHAHAHAHAHAHA!!"

"HAHAHAHAHAHAHA!! I HAVE RETURNED TO THIS WORLD NOW I WILL HAVE MY REVENGE!" After he appeared and spoke them the village elder knew that it was time to put the plan into action; DESTROY HEROBRINE FOREVER!!

Alex was still a little unclear as to what the plan was so she had them explain it one more time. "The plan is to trap him in the golems magical shield and then allow you to battle him. If you should fail his wrath will be terrible, but we will be behind you supplying you with magic abilities and healing." The elder explained. Alex was nervous but knew what would happen to the villagers and golems if she didn't.

Herobrines house had reappeared

ex saw Herobrines house reappear in the distance and told them now

s the time to strike!

On the inside of the wall, Alex stood ready for Herobrines attack.

"COME AT ME HEROBRINE! I'M READY FOR YOU!"

Alex waited for him to appear when out of nowhere she heard.

"HAHAHAHAHAHAHAAAAA!! You think I will be fooled twice by your tricks? I am not so stupid as to fall for this!"

Alex wasn't ready for Herobrines sudden attack and had to block his

ncoming attack. Without any warning or signal, the golems jumped out

f the shadows and trapped Herobrine in their magic. Alex seeing this

apt into battle with him with a mighty swing of her sword! Herobrine

asn't ready for the golems to leap out and focused on ending Alex. The

llagers seeing an opening jumped out as well and began damaging

erobrine with splash potions and poisons. They also healed Alex

rough it like they had promised and made sure she never took a hit

m Herobrine.

Herobrine's rage grew beyond belief and he started his attack!

Alex was swinging her sword when suddenly she was teleported

Alex wasn't sure what had happened only that it had happened. Looking

down at the field she saw Herobrine fall to the ground and start

screaming.

Not knowing what was happening Alex jumped down and ran to the village elder for an explanation. The elder wasn't sure what was happening but he knew it was powerful magic. "Nobody has ever defeated Herobrine completely, just banished him into different places. If this is his end I do not know what will happen." After he said this, Herobrine let out a scream that made even the golems cover their ears. In a flash of light Herobrine vanished.

"AAAAAAHHHHHH!!!!!"

The aftermath of Herobrine

Herobrine, the most feared person in Minecraft had been defeated.

No one knows exactly what happened to Herobrine after the magic

explosion; all they knew was that he was gone for good. At least that

was their hope anyways. Herobrine was defeated and it was even

confirmed by the creator. 'Herobrine removed' was the final word for

him… Or so we thought.

Alex went on with her life in Minecraft just like any other day, building, gardening, mining, and fighting zombies! Day after day she did this not even thinking of Herobrine or the battle that took place between them. Until one day when there was a huge explosion in the village near her house. Alex ran there to see what was happening and when she arrived was afraid of what it meant.

An end portal appeared in the village and Alex knew this wasn't going to end well for anyone.

Out of the distance Alex heard something that chilled her to her very

soul. A laughter that made even the mightiest of warriors fail.

erobrine had returned and he had brought an Ender Dragon to the

erworld to destroy the villagers and golems. Alex was more afraid

an she had ever been before, not only was she going to fight Herobrine

e had to fight an Ender Dragon as well. She had no plan or any idea of

at she was going to do, all she knew was she was going to do it.

Made in the USA
Middletown, DE
12 December 2014